THE SKELETON HORSE

THE UNOFFICIAL ANIMAL WARRIORS
OF THE OVERWORLD SERIES

THE SKELETON
HORSE

AN UNOFFICIAL MINECRAFTERS NOVEL
BOOK THREE

Maya Grace

Sky Pony Press
New York

THE UNOFFICIAL ANIMAL WARRIORS OF THE OVERWORLD
SERIES: THE SKELETON HORSE.

Copyright © 2019 by Hollan Publishing, Inc.

Minecraft® is a registered trademark of Notch Development AB.

The Minecraft game is copyright © Mojang AB.

Sky Pony Press books may be purchased in bulk at special discounts for sales
promotion, corporate gifts, fund-raising, or educational purposes. Special
editions can also be created to specifications. For details, contact the Special
Sales Department, Sky Pony Press, 307 West 36th Street, 11th Floor,
New York, NY 10018 or info@skyhorsepublishing.com.

Sky Pony® is a registered trademark of Skyhorse Publishing, Inc.®,
a Delaware corporation.

Visit our website at www.skyponypress.com.

10 9 8 7 6 5 4 3 2 1

Library of Congress Cataloging-in-Publication Data is available on file.

Special thanks to Erin L. Falligant.

Cover illustration by Amanda Brack
Cover design by Brian Peterson

Paperback ISBN: 978-1-5107-4135-5
Ebook ISBN: 978-1-5107-4140-9

Printed in the United States of America

TABLE OF CONTENTS

THE SKELETON HORSE

CHAPTER 1

"**N**ow, Jack!"

As Gran removed her hand from the ocelot's side, Jack carefully poured a trickle of apple-red splash potion onto the wound. Ella smelled the faint scent of melon as bubbles rose from the healing potion.

The spotted tabby cat lifted her head, mewed, and set it back down with a sigh.

"It's okay, Lucky." Jack nestled in beside her in front of the hearth.

"Give her some space," warned Gran. "An injured animal sometimes acts like a wild one."

But Ella watched as Jack carefully rested his hand on Lucky's back. The ocelot was a tamed cat now—she belonged to Jack, just as she had belonged to his mother many years ago. As Jack leaned over to whisper something in her ear, she lifted her head to lick his hand.

He can talk to her, thought Ella, *just like I can talk to Taiga.* From across the room, her grey wolf whined in response.

"Now what do we do?" asked red-headed Rowan from her seat at the kitchen table. Her knee bounced impatiently.

"Now we wait," said Gran. "She's carried that arrow for eight years. It'll take time for the wound to heal." Gran gestured toward the broken arrow she had pulled from Lucky's side.

Eight years since the Uprising, thought Ella. *Since the day-night cycle stopped and hostile mobs roamed uncontrollably across the Overworld. Since our parents . . . died.* She swallowed the lump in her throat. She and her cousins, Rowan and Jack, had lived with Gran ever since.

Ella felt a cold nose nudge her hand. Taiga seemed to sense whenever she was sad, which was often these days. *Because it's all beginning again,* thought Ella with a shiver.

She glanced outside the kitchen window, where darkness lay like a heavy blanket. The day and night cycle had almost come to a stop, except for a tiny sliver of daylight that passed across the Overworld at high noon before shadows chased it away again.

The beacon in the courtyard was on nearly all the time now, but hostile mobs grunted and groaned from beyond the mansion's walls. If Ella cocked her head, she could hear them—moaning zombies and hissing creepers. It was all Gran's iron golem could do to keep them at bay.

When a hostile mob squealed, Taiga's ears pricked. He let out a ferocious bark and raced toward the front door.

Jack jumped up from Lucky's side.

"Don't let him out!" cried Ella, lunging from her chair.

Jack's face fell. "I wasn't going to!" he said. "I know better."

"Of course you do," said Gran gently. "Taiga can go out when the sun comes up."

"Is it coming?" Rowan asked, craning her neck to see out the window.

Ella shook her head. "Not yet." But the clock on the wall showed the moon sinking low in a black sky.

During the few minutes of sunshine that would be here soon, some of the undead mobs would burn. But the sun didn't show itself every day. There had been so many clouds and storms lately!

Ella stared at the clock, willing the moon on the clock to sink lower. *Faster.*

"Taiga's right to want to fight the mobs though," Gran said solemnly. "We'll all need to fight one day soon." She finished weaving her long white hair into a tight braid, as if getting ready for battle.

Ella's stomach clenched. As she locked eyes with Rowan, she saw how *excited* Rowan looked about the idea of fighting mobs. Rowan was a warrior, like her father had been.

Even Jack puffed up a bit from his spot on the rug. "I brewed a new potion," he told Gran. "I'll show you!"

He reached for his backpack, which he always kept stocked with potions, just in case.

Gran has been preparing us for this, Ella reminded herself. She'd been preparing them for the day when they would leave the mansion and head into the Overworld, summoning armies of animals to fight the undead mobs—just as their parents had done before them.

I've been preparing for this too, enchanting weapons and armor, thought Ella. So why didn't she feel as ready as Rowan and Jack seemed to be?

As Taiga leaned into her side, she had her answer. Because fighting would put her wolf in danger. Fighting would put them *all* in danger, just as it had their parents. *And our parents didn't survive,* thought Ella. She fought down the wave of panic rising in her chest.

Beside her, Jack lined up his potion bottles like a colorful picket fence. "Potions of Slowing, Swiftness, Night Vision, Healing, Fire Resistance, Water Breathing . . . Wait, where's my new one?" He dug deep into his backpack and produced a bottle filled with lime-green liquid. "Ta-da! Potion of luck."

Gran glanced over his shoulder. "I don't know that one. Did you learn about it in your mother's journal?"

Jack nodded. His most prized possession was a dog-eared journal filled with potion-brewing recipes that his mother, a scientist, had left for him. "It gives you good luck," he said. As he flipped through the worn pages of the journal to show Gran, Ella felt a twinge of envy. She had nothing left of her own mother except a faded photo.

But Gran had said that Ella was *like* her mother— they were both wolf-whisperers. And both brave, when they needed to be. *You'll lead a great army of wolves one day, just like your mother did,* Gran often said.

Remembering those words made Ella sit up taller. But when Rowan leaped out of her chair, Ella's heart nearly stopped. "What?" she cried.

Rowan pointed toward the window. "Sunlight." She breathed the word more than said it, and smiled.

As the girls raced toward the front door, Gran called them back. "Take your jackets!"

Ella sighed. She didn't want anything to come between her skin and that glorious sunshine. But Gran was right—it would be chilly outside after hours of nightfall. She grabbed her purple jacket.

"Be careful," Gran warned. "Watch for spiders!"

The hairy-legged mobs were the only ones that could scale the courtyard wall or drop down from the roof above. When they did, Rowan took them out with a quick arrow from her bow—and Jack was usually there to scoop up the spider drops for his potions.

But today, as Ella glanced over her shoulder, she saw that Jack was staying behind with Lucky. The cat sat upright now, gently licking her wound. That meant Jack's potion was working. Ella blew out a breath of relief and then hurried after Rowan into the courtyard.

Taiga raced past Ella's feet toward the obsidian wall,

where a spindly vine ladder hung. Not long ago, Ella had been scared to climb it. But now, it offered her only view of the Overworld. And every day, that view changed. More hostile mobs roamed the hillsides. More burned-out barns and farm fields dotted the horizon. More death and destruction.

As Ella hoisted herself up onto the wall beside Rowan, she sucked in her breath. "It looks like the Nether out there," she whispered.

Small fires blazed *everywhere*—remnants of the skeletons and zombies that had burned at the first hint of daylight. A few fires lined the base of the wall below. Had zombies been knocking against it, trying to get in? Ella shivered, grateful for the obsidian Gran had used to build the house and courtyard.

Suddenly, Rowan grabbed her arm, jolting her to attention. "Look!" She pointed toward a plume of smoke on the hillside. A herd of zombies staggered through the haze. But they couldn't have been zombies—zombies would have burned with the sun. Ella looked again. "Zombie pigmen?" she whispered.

Rowan nodded. "There are more and more of them every day. More skeletons, too. And creepers. And Endermen. We have to get out there and start fighting back. I need to find my horse!"

Rowan didn't speak to wolves or ocelots, but she could communicate with horses. And one day soon, Gran said, Rowan would tame a wild horse of her own.

Not soon enough, thought Ella, watching anticipation flicker in her cousin's eyes.

"I'm ready to fight," Rowan said, more to herself than to anyone.

"Me, too," said Ella, trying to keep her voice from wobbling. "I can hear the wolves." If she tilted her head toward the forest, she could hear the howling, just as she'd heard Taiga calling to her months ago. "They're ready, too. They're ready to fight."

A shadow of envy swept across Rowan's face. Was she jealous of Ella's "army" of wolves?

"Gran said we have to tame horses *first*," Rowan pointed out. "So that we can travel faster—and more safely. You're going to have to tame a horse, too, you know."

Ella looked away. "I know that." She'd ridden a horse before, but only on a saddle behind Rowan— brave Rowan who somehow knew how to tame and ride horses without ever having been taught.

The thought of taming a horse sent a wave of anxiety through Ella's chest. Every time she pictured it, the vision ended with Ella hitting the ground. She made a mental note to enchant some boots with Feather Falling, to break her fall. Then she changed the subject. "Can you hear your horse?"

A slow smile spread across Rowan's face. "I can hear him. He's waiting for me."

Ella closed her eyes and listened, wondering if she'd be able to hear the horse, too. But she heard something else instead.

A soft *hiss,* which grew louder with each passing second.

She opened her eyes as the hissing creeper rounded the corner of the wall below.

Then she ducked her head and gripped the wall—just in time.

Boom!

CHAPTER 2

As Taiga barked and whined from the courtyard below, Ella opened her eyes. Gunpowder swirled around her like snowflakes.

Rowan clung to the wall beside Ella. "Are you okay?" she asked, coughing.

Ella nodded. She leaned forward just enough to be sure the creeper hadn't blown a hole in the obsidian wall. *It didn't,* she assured herself. *We're safe.* But suddenly, Gran's courtyard didn't feel so safe.

Taiga barked so wildly from below that Ella had no choice but to climb down. As she slid down the vine ladder, her hands burned.

"Girls, are you all right?" Gran hurried toward them.

"Just a creeper." Rowan sounded bored, as if she were talking about an annoying silverfish. "At least it wasn't super-charged."

Ella had never seen a super-charged creeper, one that had been struck by lightning. Just the thought made her legs feel shaky. As the sun sank in the sky and shadows spilled across the courtyard, her spirits did, too.

"That settles it," said Gran. "It's time to hide our valuables and pack our things. It's time to go—before it's too late."

"Our valuables?" said Ella. The only valuable thing she had was pacing the ground in front of her, whining. She leaned forward to pull Taiga into a hug. "Yes, you're coming, too," she whispered into his fur.

Click!

The beacon suddenly lit up the courtyard, powered by a daylight sensor. But as the Overworld beyond plunged again into darkness, Ella heard the scuttle of spider legs climbing the wall. She quickly followed Gran back inside.

* * *

"Take only what's most precious to you," said Gran. "What won't weigh you down."

Ella hoisted her backpack. It was heavy, yes. But what weighed her down most of all was sadness—the realization that even if they fought this great battle and actually won, they might still not have a house to come home to. Gran had just said so.

"Our house is made of obsidian," Jack protested, looking younger than he actually was. "Nothing could destroy it!"

Gran shook her head. "That's not true. The house has protected us for many years, but we've protected it, too. If we're not here to keep the torches lit inside, mobs could spawn. Everything could be destroyed."

"My books," Ella whispered. She hadn't thought of them until now—an entire shelf in the Enchantment Room, devoted to enchantments that she might need *someday.*

Gran shook her head again. "I'm sorry, Ella. We can't take them with us—only the enchanted items we think we'll need."

Jack threw his arm around her. "It'll be okay, Ella," he said. "I'll find you more, just like the one I found hidden in the chest in the jungle temple."

He *had* found the book enchanted with Loyalty, which Ella had used to enchant the trident she was packing for their journey. But it would take a lot of chests in a lot of temples to make up for the number of books she'd be leaving behind. "Thanks," she said. But it was hard to muster a smile.

"Wait," said Rowan, holding up her hand. "Can we hide the books? And other things? You know, like Jack said—the way treasures were hidden in the temple."

Gran hesitated. "We could . . . but there's only room for a few things. I'll show you."

As she led them down the cobblestone steps to the basement, Ella's heart raced. The only room at the base of the stairs was Jack's potion-brewing room. There wasn't a chest in there. So where was Gran taking them?

Halfway down the stairs, she stopped. She studied

the wall, as if trying to remember. Then she pulled the pickaxe from her belt and pried one of the stones loose from the wall.

As it gave way, Ella jumped backward, expecting silverfish. Instead, the stone hid an entryway—a dark tunnel.

"Grab the torch," Gran said to Rowan.

Rowan reached up and took the torch from the wall. "Can I go first?"

Gran nodded. "But be careful."

In a flash, Rowan disappeared into the tunnel. Ella held her breath, watching the flickering torchlight bounce around the tunnel. Then she heard Rowan call out.

"Cool! Guys, get in here!"

Jack climbed through next, and then Gran waved her hand toward the tunnel. "Your turn, dear," she said to Ella.

Here goes nothing, thought Ella, putting on a brave face. As she started to crawl through the narrow corridor, cobwebs brushed against her skin and tickled her nose. When the tunnel opened up and she could finally stand, she sucked in her breath.

Two chests rested against the back wall of a tiny room. Between them sat a strange block with buttons. Rowan had already flung open one chest and was pulling out books and photos. "My dad!" she said, holding up a photo of a man dressed in armor.

But Jack studied something else. "What's this?" he asked as Gran's head popped out of the tunnel. He pointed toward the block between the chests.

Gran's eyes widened. "Goodness," she said, "I haven't thought about that in years. It's a command block, something your mother was building. Oh, and Rowan, you found some treasures, too."

When she saw the photo Rowan was holding, Gran's eyes welled with tears. "Wasn't he handsome?" she said, reaching out to stroke the photo. "This is where we hid our most precious things before the last Uprising."

As Gran opened the other trunk, Ella stepped up to see what was inside. Something glittered—a diamond chestplate. And beneath that, a sack of apples.

"Golden apples!" Jack cried. "And so many of them."

Gran nodded. "Your mother liked to craft those," she said.

"For healing zombie villagers?" asked Jack.

Rowan scoffed. "There's no such thing," she said. "That's just a rumor."

"It's not!" said Jack. "Villagers killed by zombies can sometimes turn into zombie villagers. I read about them in Mom's journal—she wrote down the cure. We should bring some golden apples with us."

He had said *some,* but Ella saw Jack put every last apple into his backpack. She stood on tiptoe to search the corners of the chest. Was there anything in there for her?

Then she saw them—glistening white skeleton bones. "My mom's?" she asked Gran as she reached for a bone. It felt smooth beneath her fingertips.

Gran nodded. "For taming wolves," she said with a smile.

When Gran said the diamond chestplate had belonged to Rowan's father, Rowan put it right on. It was big and loose, but as soon as she had tightened it around her waist, she beamed like the courtyard beacon.

"So this is where you can hide your books, Ella," said Gran. "And anything else that you kids want to be sure stays safe."

For just a moment, Ella wanted to climb into the chest herself. And close the lid. And stay in there forever—or at least until Gran, Rowan, and Jack returned to say that they'd beaten the undead mobs. That the Overworld had been set right again.

But instead, she closed the lid with a creak. "I'll get my books," she said, climbing back into the dark tunnel before anyone could see the worry clouding her eyes.

CHAPTER 3

"I can't see!" Ella squinted into the darkness, trying to keep up with Rowan's glittery armor as she led the way across the dark field.

"Jack, give her more potion," called Gran from behind.

When Ella stopped, Jack bumped right into her, his armor clanking. But as Ella took a swig of the carrot-flavored potion of night vision, she was grateful to Jack. Without him, she'd be blind as a bat in this darkness. Gran was saving the torches for later, when they would hopefully find shelter and try to sleep.

As Jack crouched down to return the bottle to his backpack, Ella's heart squeezed. He looked tiny in his oversized armor. Ella had enchanted the armor with Unbreaking, but would it be enough to protect him?

She shook her head, trying to shake off the worry. Jack had proven that he could take care of himself. He had journeyed alone to the jungle to find his ocelot, and he had survived—thanks to his potions. *He'll survive this, too,* Ella assured herself. But she started walking slower, making sure Jack could keep up.

As the potion took effect, Ella's eyes adjusted. Now she could see Rowan clear as day up ahead, her diamond chestplate twinkling in the moonlight. Rowan held her horse saddle out in front of her like a shield, and kept her ears trained for the whinny of the horse she hoped to tame.

Instead, they heard the low groan of a zombie— and a few grunts. Wherever the zombie had spawned, it was not alone. "Where are they?" As Ella swung her head side to side, Taiga growled at her feet.

"Shh," said Gran in a steady voice. "We can outrun zombies. Don't fight unless you have to."

Rowan whirled around. "Wait, what? I thought that was our goal—to kill hostile mobs. Isn't that why we're out here?"

"We're out here to build an army," said Gran firmly, "so that we don't have to fight alone. The sun will take care of the zombies—as long as we still have a sliver of sunlight each day. So save your potions and your weapons. Steer clear of the zombies, and stay calm."

Stay calm? How? Ella quickened her pace—and up ahead, Rowan did, too.

"Good girl," Jack crooned into the darkness.

For just a moment, Ella wondered if he was talking to her. Then she remembered the ocelot that was trailing Jack.

"Ocelots keep creepers away, right, Gran?" he asked.

"That's right," said Gran. "Lucky is going to be our good-luck charm."

Suddenly, Rowan stopped walking and dropped her gaze toward the ground. "Do ocelots keep Endermen away, too?" she whispered.

Ella looked up—just long enough to catch the purple eyes glowing from a few yards away.

"Don't look!" Gran warned. "Ignore him, and he'll ignore us."

Ella forced her legs to keep moving and her eyes to look down instead of up. But her heart thudded in her ears. "Stay calm," she whispered to Taiga. "We're not going to fight unless we have to."

Taiga whined, but he did as he was told.

"Good boy," she whispered.

Finally, they'd made it over the hilltop—and the Enderman hadn't teleported toward them. Ella blew out a breath she hadn't known she'd been holding, just as thunder rumbled overhead.

"No!" Rowan cried. "Not a storm. Not now!"

Gran caught up with her. "The rain will take care of the Endermen," she said. "And we'll find shelter soon."

"But my horse!" Rowan cried.

"Your horse will wait for you," said Gran, reaching for Rowan's arm. "It's time to look for shelter."

Jack spotted the farm first, which made Ella wonder if he'd been sneaking extra potion of night vision. The farm had been abandoned for a while—Ella could tell by the dried-up crops in the fields, the broken fence line, and the burned-out structure that had once been a house. What had happened to the farmer? Ella tried not to think about that as she followed Rowan toward the barn.

"Wait!" called Gran. "Watch for mobs inside."

That's when a crack of lightning lit up the sky, and the clouds opened up. As rain poured down, Rowan *didn't* wait—she pushed open the barn door. And then screamed.

Ella heard the *thwack* of Rowan's bow and then a grunt. By the time Ella made it inside, Rowan had dropped the zombie with a single arrow. She was standing over the mob, looking victorious.

"Well done, Rowan," said Gran as she stepped into the darkness of the barn. "Did the zombie drop anything?"

Rowan studied the ground and wrinkled her nose. "Carrots and potatoes."

"Gather them up, girls," said Gran. "You never know when our food supply might run low."

As Ella stepped over a steamy mound of rotten flesh, her stomach turned. She gathered a few potatoes, still warm to the touch, and put them in Gran's canvas sack.

As thunder rumbled overhead and raindrops beat against the roof of the barn, Gran lit a torch. Soon, hay bales were arranged like beds. With Taiga beside her, Ella could almost close her eyes and imagine that she was back home in Gran's mansion. *Almost.*

But when a crack of lightning hit the ground nearby, she sprang off the hay. Taiga did, too.

"Did it hit the barn?" asked Rowan.

Gran was already running toward the barn door. "Let's hope not," she said. "We don't need any more fires." She pushed it open, just a little, to check the ground outside.

That's when Taiga tore through the gap and disappeared into the darkness.

CHAPTER 4

Ella didn't think—she just ran. Out of the barn. Into the darkness. Into the storm.

The potion of night vision had worn off long ago, and she could see nothing—except for a blinding beacon up ahead. She stumbled toward it, ignoring Gran's calls to come back.

"Taiga!" Ella cried. She listened for his bark, but heard nothing.

As she fumbled toward the blue beacon, she suddenly realized that it was moving. Toward her. And that it wasn't a beacon at all.

The barn hadn't been struck by lightning. A *creeper* had! And the super-charged creeper was about to blow.

Ella whirled around to race back toward the barn. *But I can't!* she realized. *I'll lead the creeper right back to my family!*

Instead, she raced past him, giving the creeper a

wide berth. And then Taiga was at her heels, barking and snapping at the creeper.

"No!" Ella cried. "Don't get too close to it!"

She felt the explosion before she heard it. The hairs on her arms stood straight up, and then her body lifted off the ground—as if an ocean wave had reached onshore and swept her off her feet.

BOOM!!!

Her ears rang with the sound. Then she was falling. And the world went silent.

*   *   *

"Ella!"

Gran was tapping her cheek.

As Ella sat up on the hay bale, every muscle in her body ached. Then she remembered. "Taiga!"

"He's safe," said Jack. "See?"

Loyal Taiga was right there beside Ella. As he lunged forward to lick her face, Ella squeezed her eyes tight with relief.

"You're safe, too," Gran said soothingly. "Somehow."

Even Rowan looked impressed. "You didn't have a diamond chestplate," she said, stroking her own armor. "How are you not hurt?"

Ella wiggled her fingers and then her toes. "Enchanted armor," she said. Her face spread into a smile. "Enchanted with Protection." Then she glanced down at her feet. "And boots enchanted with Feather Falling."

"You really *fell*," said Jack, his eyes wide. "But wait, why didn't Lucky keep the creeper away?"

"Maybe she did," said Gran, squeezing his shoulder. "Lucky probably kept that creeper out of the barn. And *Ella* led it away from us." Gran's smile was full of gratitude—and something else. *Pride.*

Gran is proud of me, Ella realized. Her throat suddenly felt tight.

When Gran said they should try to get some rest, Ella scooted sideways so that Jack could sit next to her. She tried to think of happy things, like being back in the warm kitchen of the mansion, with Gran making applesauce and singing along to the jukebox.

But while Jack drifted off into a peaceful slumber, Ella lay awake, staring up at the shadowy rafters of the barn.

* * *

"You know what's even more cool than a super-charged creeper?" Jack asked.

Now that the rain had stopped, they were walking again, but Jack wouldn't stop talking about what had happened the night before.

"What's even more cool?" asked Ella, taking his bait.

"Skeleton horses," Jack announced. "When lightning strikes a skeleton horse, it can spawn skeleton horsemen—like three or four of them."

"What's cool about that?" Ella asked. She'd seen spider jockeys before, skeletons that ride spiders.

Somehow, the idea of a skeleton riding a skeleton horse seemed even spookier.

"Actually," said Gran, "skeleton horses are incredibly fast—most of them are faster than minecarts. If we had skeleton horses, we could cross the Overworld much more quickly."

Rowan's eyes lit up, but Ella shook her head. *No thanks,* she thought. Taming a *regular* horse was scary enough, even with her enchanted boots.

Then she saw something—a column of smoke rising over the hill. "Is that a barn on fire?"

Rowan squinted into the darkness. "How could anything be on fire during a rainstorm?" she said.

As they crested the hill, they could smell the smoke.

"There *was* a fire," Gran said solemnly. "Most likely many small fires. The storm put them out."

Now Ella could see more clearly. "That's not a barn," she cried. "That's a village!"

Gran nodded. "Indeed." But she didn't show any signs of heading downhill toward the village.

"Should we help them?" Ella asked, imagining all the villager children who had just lost their homes.

Gran hesitated, then shook her head. "It's too late. And remember, Ella—you can't help someone who believes you're the enemy."

A memory flooded Ella's mind: Gran being thrown into jail by villagers who believed she was a witch, just because Gran could communicate with animals. And it had happened before. Villagers had turned against Ella's own parents during the last Uprising.

It could happen again, Ella knew. *To us—Rowan, Jack, and me—because we talk with animals, too.* She reached down to give Taiga a squeeze.

"How did the fires start?" Jack asked. His eyes were so wide now, Ella could nearly see the burned-out village reflected inside.

"Probably a zombie siege," said Rowan as she tightened her grip on her bow. "Zombies pour into a village, burst into flames at daybreak, and then burn down the whole village with them. Right, Gran?"

Gran didn't have to nod. Ella could tell by the expression on her face that Rowan had gotten it right. So where were the villagers now? Had they burned in their own homes? Or had they been driven out into the night, where mobs had destroyed them?

Ella scanned the hillsides, wondering if any villagers had survived—*hoping* that some had survived.

Then she heard the whinny of a horse.

CHAPTER 5

"**R**owan!" Ella raced after her cousin into the darkness, but her armor weighed her down.

Rowan had run through a thin patch of trees. Ella followed, dodging branches and ducking under limbs. When she finally broke through into a clearing, she stopped with a jolt.

Brave, red-headed Rowan stood in the clearing—in the middle of a herd of horses.

Taiga whined, circling Ella's feet.

"No!" Ella whispered. "Stay here. Those horses are *wild*."

None of the horses had saddles. None had bridles or ropes. Ella could see the whites of their eyes and practically smell their fear. As Rowan made her way through the herd, the horses whinnied and sidestepped away from her.

Except for one.

The cocoa-brown bay studied Rowan just as intently as she studied him. When she took a step closer and held out her hand, the horse nickered and shook his mane.

"It's okay," Rowan said soothingly. "Remember me? I've been waiting for you for so long now."

Is this Rowan's horse? Ella wondered. She watched as Rowan stepped closer. She reached up to stroke the horse's neck, which gleamed in the moonlight. He snorted, blowing out a hot breath of air.

But when Rowan stepped closer still, he lowered his head toward hers. He smelled her hair. And then he sighed, as if giving in.

Rowan pulled the horse's head gently downward, into a hug. Then, smooth as can be, she tied a lead rope around his neck.

"Ella!" Gran's voice broke the magic of the moment. "Get the saddle!" Gran pointed toward Rowan's saddle, which sat at the edge of the clearing.

"Me?" Ella's voice rang out so sharply, every horse in the clearing turned to stare. One stomped the ground, as if warning her to stay away. How could Ella carry a saddle through a herd of wild horses?

"Rowan needs it!" Gran explained. "To tame the horse."

But Ella's feet felt rooted to the earth. So Gran did it herself. She lifted the saddle and carried it toward the horses. Was she whispering something to them? Ella strained to hear. Whatever Gran was saying worked— the horses stepped away, clearing a path for her.

As Gran handed Rowan the saddle, she took the lead rope from Rowan to hold the horse still. Then Rowan ever so slowly raised the saddle onto his back. She tightened the saddle and then reached for the horn.

As Rowan pulled herself onto the horse's back, Gran darted safely aside—and Ella sucked in her breath. She felt Jack's hand slide into hers and heard twigs snapping overhead. His ocelot was up there in the branches, watching too.

Instantly, Rowan's horse reared. But she hung on tight. "It's okay," she told him. "It's all right. You know me, remember?"

The horse settled down into a trot, carving a wide circle around the clearing. He bucked only once more. By the time Rowan had ridden him all the way around, back toward Jack and Ella, the horse was hers—Ella could tell.

"You did it!" Ella cried.

"I did it." Rowan wrapped her arms around her horse's neck and squeezed tightly.

"What's his name?" asked Jack.

Rowan smiled. "Victory," she said, as if it were the sweetest word she knew. "Because that's what he's going to bring us. Victory is going to lead the way."

Victory nickered in agreement.

Rowan stroked his mane lovingly and gave his neck a pat. Then she sat up straight. "Your turn to tame a horse," she announced.

When Ella realized her cousin was staring at her, her stomach dropped. "I can't," she said.

"You *can*," said Rowan. "Watch Gran."

Ella swiveled just in time to see Gran throw a lead rope around the neck of a chestnut-colored horse. She made it look so easy! *But Gran doesn't have a saddle,* Ella realized. *Can she tame the horse without one?*

Ella watched in amazement as Gran led the horse toward a tree stump. She stepped up onto the stump and then quick as a flash, mounted the horse—bareback.

The chestnut horse reared, trying to toss Gran off. It bucked wildly, trying to shake her off its rear.

"It's going to hurt Gran!" cried Jack.

Taiga whined and panted, willing Ella to let him go help their grandmother.

"No!" Ella cried. "The horse will trample you!" But would it trample Gran, too?

Again and again the chestnut horse bucked. But Gran hung on. *Finally,* the horse quieted down. Ella saw the moment when it relaxed its muscles, sighed, and lowered its head. *Yes!*

Gran slid off its back and led the horse toward Jack and Ella. Gran was still breathing heavily, and her forehead glistened with sweat. But her grey eyes shone bright. "Do you want to ride her?" she asked Ella. "Or will you tame your own?"

Ella knew what Gran wanted her to say. *Yes, I'll tame one! Of course I will!* But as her gaze drifted back to those wild horses, fear bucked in her chest.

Gran must have noticed. Was that a flicker of disappointment in her eyes? She held the rope toward Ella. "The mare will be tough to control without a saddle," said Gran. "We'll need to find one soon. But until then, I think she'll follow Rowan's horse wherever we go."

The chestnut mare was already straining at the rope, eager to follow Victory.

Ella reached for the rope, grateful that she wouldn't have to tame a horse of her own. But as something whizzed overhead, the horse reared, ripping the rope from Ella's hands.

Gran ran for the horse. Jack let loose a shriek. And Ella turned to see a spider jockey stepping out of the woods.

The spider's eyes glowed red, and the skeleton on its back had raised its bow again.

And pointed its sharp-tipped arrow.

Directly at Ella.

CHAPTER 6

"**C**limb on!"

As Victory galloped out of the darkness, Rowan swooped down from the saddle and offered Ella her hand.

Without thinking, Ella grabbed it. She grasped the saddle with her other hand and scrambled onto Victory's back, just as a barrage of arrows flew overhead.

"More spider jockeys!" cried Gran. She had already pulled Jack up to safety on her chestnut mare.

But what about Taiga? Ella's heart clutched with fear. Could the wolf keep up—without getting hit by a skeleton arrow?

There was no time to think. Spiders were crawling out of the trees now, spilling off branches. As they dropped to the ground below, the bony jockeys on their backs raised their bows.

"Shoot back!" Rowan cried. "Use my bow!"

Ella reached for it. But how could she hang on to Rowan with one hand and fire off an arrow with the other? She couldn't! Instead, she pulled the trident from her waist. The three-pronged spear was heavy, but Gran had taught her how to throw it like a spear.

Ella spun around at the waist and suddenly realized that Gran and Jack were right behind her—the chestnut mare was following Victory, nose to tail. Then Ella saw the spider jockey ride up beside Gran, its bow raised.

"Look out!" Ella cried. But Gran couldn't fight back. She was riding bareback, hanging on to the horse's mane—and to Jack—for dear life. She shot Ella a look that said, *Do something—fast!*

Jack was *trying* to do something. He used his teeth to pull a cork out of a bottle of splash potion. *But there's no time,* thought Ella.

She raised her arm and whipped the trident at the spider jockey. As it zoomed past the skeleton and plummeted toward the ground below, her stomach dropped with it. But the trident distracted the skeleton. He lowered his bow.

Ella had to strike again—*now*. She held her hand open, waiting. She had enchanted the trident with Loyalty, which meant that it would come back to her, as loyal as Taiga the wolf. Ella's heart hurt at the thought of her wolf. *Please let him be okay!*

Smack! The trident was back in her hand, ready for another throw. But Victory was racing through the forest now, dodging trees and low-hanging branches. Ella wobbled from side to side on the horse's back, desperate to hang on.

"Duck!" cried Rowan.

Ella did, just in time to miss the branch that could have knocked her off the horse.

As they sped deeper into the dark forest, she kept her head low and her mind focused on one thought: *Please let us make it out of here alive—and my loyal wolf, too.*

* * *

"High noon," said Gran, staring upward as she tied her horse's rope to the trunk of a birch tree.

Ella glanced up quickly. But the canopy of trees was so thick overhead, she could barely see the cracks of sunlight shining through. She wished she could fly to the top, quick as a bird, and raise her face toward the sky. Then she would part the branches and search for Taiga. Where *was* he?

She slid off the back of Rowan's horse and called again. "Taiga!"

From atop Gran's horse, Jack called out, too. "Lucky!"

Their voices rang off the tree trunks and came right back, like tridents.

"Listen for your animals," said Gran. "You know how."

Ella nodded. She squeezed her eyes shut and listened with her heart and her mind, not only with her ears. She heard a wolf howling, and then two or three others. A pack of wolves howled mournfully. But not one of them was Taiga.

She opened her eyes, avoiding Gran's questioning glance. "I don't hear him," she said softly. But what did that mean? Had something happened to her wolf? Fear pricked the back of her neck.

"I don't hear Lucky either," Jack mumbled. "I wish I had a potion of hearing."

Rowan cocked her head and gazed off into the distance. "I hear wolves—they're howling, I think. Why can't you hear them, Ella?"

Ella shook her head. "I *do* hear them, but they're not Taiga."

"They're still your wolves," said Gran. "We need them to help us fight, remember?"

Ella swallowed the lump in her throat and nodded.

"Can you tell where they are?" asked Gran.

Ella squeezed her eyes shut again. This time, she not only heard the howling wolves, but she also saw them—trotting along a dirt path through the forest. The lead wolf stopped and turned back, howling at the others to keep up. Beside him, Ella saw what looked like a giant . . . mushroom.

She chuckled. "That can't be right."

"What?" said Gran. "Tell me what you see."

As Ella described the giant red mushroom, tall as tree, Jack's eyes widened. "I'd like to see a mushroom like that," he said. Ella was pretty sure she heard his stomach growl.

"Maybe we will," said Gran, gazing thoughtfully down the forest path. "Giant mushrooms grow in the Roofed Forest. We're nearly there. We may have our army of wolves before you know it!" Her gray eyes flashed as she quickly untied the horse.

Ella saw the shadow cross Rowan's face again, at the mention of that army of wolves. "We'll need more horses too, right?" asked Rowan.

Gran shook her head. "Just a saddle," she said. "I'm too old to be riding bareback." She rubbed her backside and winced.

But Rowan wouldn't let it go. "We should each have our own horse," she insisted. She stared at Ella as if to say, *You need to tame your own, scaredy-cat.*

Irritation bubbled up inside Ella, like a pot of mushroom stew. She stared right back. "We don't need more horses—Gran said so. They don't fight off mobs the way wolves do."

Rowan's cheeks turned crimson. "Maybe not, but at least my horse outran those mobs."

Her words struck Ella's heart like a lightning bolt. Was Rowan saying that Taiga *didn't* outrun the mobs?

Ella took a step backward and reached for a tree to steady herself. She wouldn't believe it—and she'd never forgive Rowan for saying those words out loud.

Gran stepped between them and held out her hands. "Girls, we have an Overworld of hostile mobs to fight," she said sternly. "Let's not fight among ourselves."

Still, Ella wouldn't look at Rowan. *Forget her,* she

thought sourly. *I'll pretend she drank a potion of invisibility. I'll look after Jack and Gran instead.*

But as her eyes darted back toward Jack, she saw him looking skyward.

She heard the snap of a branch overhead.

And something lunged downward, straight toward Jack.

CHAPTER 7

In a flash, Ella grabbed her trident. But her cousin beat her to it. Rowan had her bow raised in seconds, and an arrow in place—ready to strike. Ready to take down the hostile mob that had just wound itself around Jack's legs.

And licked his hand.

"Lucky!" Jack squealed, dropping to the ground beside his ocelot. "You're alive! You found me!"

Ella blew out the adrenaline that had just coursed through her body, and tried to ignore the envy that crept along after it.

Jack had his cat back. His loyal cat. And Ella was happy about that—really she was! *But my wolf is still out there somewhere,* she thought sadly. *At least I hope he is.*

Gran stepped around Lucky, checking for any injuries. "She's alright," said Gran. "Well done, Lucky." She stroked the cat's head.

But Lucky only had eyes for Jack. She rubbed against him again and again, purring so loudly that Ella swore she could feel the ground rumbling.

"Gran, are there ocelots in the Roofed Forest, too?" Jack asked suddenly. "Can Lucky and I gather an army of our own?"

Rowan scoffed at that. "You can only find ocelots in the jungle, Jack."

Gran shrugged. "There may be some out here—you never know. Day has turned to night. The Overworld has turned upside down. So, you never know." She winked at Jack, whose eyes lit up at the thought of taming more ocelots.

But Rowan's mood grew darker, Ella could tell. Was she jealous of Jack now, too, because he might gather an army of ocelots?

As Ella climbed back onto Victory, she reached for the saddle instead of Rowan's hand. And as they started back along the thickly wooded trail, she stayed silent. Rowan said nothing, either. Every so often, she clucked her tongue, urging Victory to go faster.

Lulled by the rhythm of the trotting horse, Ella closed her eyes, listening for wolves. She could see more of them now in her mind. But instead of howling mournfully, they paced the forest trail, waiting.

Waiting for me? she wondered. *What will I do when I find them? How can I lead them without Taiga by my side?*

The only thing that took Ella's mind off of her wolf were the huge mushrooms that had begun to appear, mixed in with the oak trees on either side of the trail. "There's a brown one!" cried Jack. "Ooh, and a red!"

When Ella turned to look, she caught him reaching from the back of the mare and scooping a handful of mushroom off the nearest plant. He shoved it into his mouth before Gran could see.

"Ew, Jack! We should cook it first," said Ella, busting him. "My sword's enchanted with Fire Aspect, remember?"

Jack stopped chewing. He puffed out his cheeks and spit the mushroom into a bush.

"Gross!" cried Ella. But the thought of warm mushroom stew made her stomach clench with hunger. When had they last eaten? She couldn't remember. Her enchanted sword could turn one of these mushroom "trees" into a roasted, smoky dinner in seconds flat.

Gran scolded Jack, too. "Let's spend less time wasting mushrooms and more time watching out for mobs, alright?" she said. "Keep looking up. Spiders and other mobs may drop down from the top of those giant mushrooms that are making you so hungry."

Ella glanced up, her appetite suddenly gone. She could barely *see* the top of the nearest red mushroom, let alone see if anything was on top of it. But she kept watch, knowing that Rowan had to keep her eyes on the trail ahead.

When the trail eventually split, Victory hesitated—and Rowan did, too.

"Take the right fork," Gran called from behind. "Uphill, so we can get a better view."

Rowan shifted the rope in her hand slightly, and Victory took her cue. The path upward was steep and rocky. As they passed trees, Ella fought the urge to reach out and grab the branches for safety.

From behind, Jack let out a squeal. "Hang on!" Gran urged him. "I won't let you fall."

But as Ella slid backward in her own seat, she knew that right now, Rowan probably *would* let her fall. A wall of tension separated the girls. *And it's made of obsidian,* thought Ella. How could Rowan have said something so awful about Taiga?

He can outrun a spider jockey, Ella told herself. *He can, and he did. I know it. No matter what Rowan says.*

When the trail finally leveled out, Ella glanced around. The trees had thinned now, and a moonlit clearing stretched before them filled with dandelions and other wildflowers. She instinctively scanned the clearing for mobs. Rowan gripped her bow tightly, too, as she led Victory across the clearing to the edge of a rocky cliff, with a river rushing below.

From up here, Ella saw just how dense the dark forest was below. Every so often, a lake or clearing punctuated the canopy of trees. But the thick green forest seemed to stretch on for miles. "You could get lost in there," she murmured. *Like Taiga.*

"You could," Gran agreed as her horse stepped up beside Victory.

Rowan said nothing. Her eyes were glued to something in the forest. "What's that?" she asked, pointing.

An L-shaped cobblestone building with a brown

roof rose from the forest floor, two or three stories tall. Ella could just barely count the windows—six or seven along one side of the top floor. "Is it someone's house?" she asked.

"It's not a house. It's a mansion!" cried Jack.

"That's right," said Gran. "A woodland mansion!" She sounded almost as excited as Jack.

Ella turned to face her. "Does someone live in there?"

Gran shook her head. "Maybe a few illagers—vindicators and evokers."

"Huh?" asked Ella. It was as if Gran were speaking another language. What were *illagers*?

Even Rowan looked confused.

"Hostile mobs that we'll need to contend with in the mansion," Gran explained. "But we'll also find shelter for the night, and maybe some chests with supplies, and hopefully . . . a saddle."

Her horse nickered softly, as if in agreement.

"The mansion is just past the bend in the river," said Gran. "We'll follow the river until we run into it." She studied the forest below, as if memorizing the route they would take.

"So what are we waiting for?" asked Rowan, who seemed to have found her voice again. She turned her horse back toward the clearing.

As they sped down the rocky trail, Ella held on tight, replaying Gran's words in her mind. *Illagers?* Ella didn't like the sound of that. It felt as if new and more hostile mobs might spring up around every bend in the trail.

But Taiga? Ella's wolf was nowhere to be found.

*   *   *

The mansion seemed even larger from ground than it had from up above. Ella sucked in her breath.

It was definitely three stories tall, with windows lining every level. Torches burned brightly on either side of the front door, as if welcoming the kids for a visit. *Or luring us toward danger,* Ella thought suddenly. *Are illagers watching us from those windows right now?* She flinched and ducked her head.

"Should we tie up the horses?" whispered Rowan.

Gran shook her head. "They'll be safer if we leave them untied."

Ella locked eyes with Rowan and saw a flicker of fear cross her cousin's face. As mad as she'd been at Rowan for the last couple of hours, she felt a stab of compassion. Rowan had waited a long time to tame Victory. She didn't want anything to happen to her horse.

Just like I don't want anything to happen to Taiga, thought Ella.

But the moment passed as quickly as it came. Rowan stood up straight, her shoulders back. "Victory won't run away," she stated, patting her horse's neck. "Right, buddy?"

He nickered a response.

"And my horse will stay close to Victory's side," Gran agreed.

"You should name her," Jack piped up. "You can't just keep calling her 'my horse.'"

Gran smiled, but kept her eyes trained on the mansion. "We can name her later, when we've found a safe place to rest. C'mon, follow me," she whispered, waving her arm.

When she reached the cobblestone staircase leading toward the front door, she pulled her sword from her side. Ella grabbed her weapon too, choosing her trident over her sword.

As Rowan pushed past with her bow drawn, Ella heard the clink of glass, which meant Jack was readying a potion. She turned just in time to see Lucky jump to the low roof of the first story of the mansion. The ocelot was going to keep watch on her boy from up above, if she could. And somehow, that made Ella feel a bit safer—and more brave.

She followed Rowan through the front door without hesitating, waiting only for Jack to catch up before tiptoeing into the dark foyer. Though the bright red carpet looked clean and new, the foyer smelled dank and musty. Ella wrinkled her nose.

Several doors led off the foyer. But instead of choosing one, Gran led them up yet another set of cobblestone stairs.

"Why are we going up?" Ella whispered, hoping Rowan would hear—but that any illagers in the mansion wouldn't.

"That's where the illagers are," said Rowan curtly. "We fight first, and then we rest." Her jaw was set in a firm line, reminding Ella of the photo of Rowan's father.

Was he always ready to fight on a moment's notice, too? Ella wondered. She longed to turn around and go back down, *away* from the hostile mobs. But Jack was glued to her back, so she kept going up, up, up . . .

. . . until they'd reached a long hallway lined with doors.

"Which one?" Rowan whispered to Gran.

Gran shrugged. "We won't know until we open them," she said. "Let's stick together."

As Gran opened a door on one side of the hall, Rowan opened a door on the other. Ella stood between them. *Keeping Jack safe,* she decided.

But Jack had already pulled out a glass bottle. "Potion of slowness," he explained to Ella. "Just in case."

"Bedroom!" Rowan announced, stepping back from the doorway so that the others could see.

As Ella gazed at the three beds, covered in cozy blue bedspreads, a wave of sleepiness washed over her. She longed to run into that room and dive straight into bed—to sleep for a day, or at least until the sun rose again. From this top-story bedroom, maybe she could see and feel the sunshine streaming in the window. She yawned sleepily, until Gran pulled the door shut.

"No resting yet," Gran said. "We have to make sure there aren't any illagers in the house first. We can't sleep unless we know we're safe."

I can, Ella wanted to argue. But then she caught

sight of what was in the open room across the hall. "Is that an anvil?"

An anvil meant enchantments. It meant Ella could take some of their weapons and armor and make them even *stronger.*

She raced into the room without thinking, without drawing her sword. When she reached the anvil, she could tell it was broken—the slot where a weapon might go was cracked, as if someone had hit it with a pickaxe.

Ella's shoulders sunk with disappointment. But as she spun around to tell Gran, she came face to face with a villager in a brown jacket. He stood with his arms crossed, blocking her path.

Ella opened her mouth to say hello, but nothing came out.

This villager was so *pale,* and his nose so large— like a witch's nose. Ella took a step backward, and ran right up against the anvil. She was trapped!

When the villager uncrossed his arms, she saw the glint of an iron axe. Seconds later, he'd raised it above his head, ready to strike. And Gran shrieked a warning.

"It's a vindicator! Ella, run!"

CHAPTER 8

Ella ducked and hit the ground. But as she rolled away from the vindicator, he sprinted toward her, raising his axe again.

Ella sprang to her feet and grabbed for her sword. But it slipped from her sweaty fingers and clattered to the ground. She couldn't reach it—not in time!

The vindicator's axe was coming down now. It moved as if in slow motion, as if time were standing still. Ella's last thought was of Taiga. *I'm sorry, buddy,* she thought, squeezing her eyes shut. *I'm sorry I couldn't find you.*

She waited for the blow of the axe—but it never came.

As she whipped open her eyes, she saw that the axe was still overhead, moving downward second by second. It *was* moving in slow motion! And broken glass lay on the floor all around.

Jack's potion of slowness! Ella spotted her cousin in the doorway, just before Gran and Rowan pushed past him into the room. Gran took out the vindicator with a single fierce strike of her sword. As Rowan watched the mob fall, she looked disappointed that she hadn't gotten in a blow, too.

But Ella collapsed to the floor in a heap of relief. She squeezed back tears, not wanting anyone to see. Then she felt Jack beside her. "Thanks, buddy," she said, pulling him into a hug. "You saved me, you know."

"I know," he said. "Just like you saved us from the super-charged creeper."

Ella laughed at that and opened her eyes. "That's why we stick together, right?"

He nodded.

"That's right," said Gran, pulling Ella to her feet. "So no more running ahead of us into rooms, alright?"

When Ella saw tears glistening in Gran's eyes, she felt a pang of guilt. She'd nearly scared Gran to death, too. But she wouldn't do it again.

As they continued down the long hall, opening doors to check for more hostile mobs, Ella stuck close to Jack and kept her sword drawn. They passed more bedrooms, some with single beds and others with double beds. But Ella wasn't sleepy anymore.

I may never sleep again, she thought to herself, after her battle with the vindicator and his axe.

"Meeting room," Gran announced, closing a door behind her.

"Library," said Rowan, closing her door, too.

"Wait, what?" Ella felt a tingle of excitement run down her spine.

Rowan shrugged. "Just bookshelves filled with books. Don't you have enough of those at home?"

"Yeah, but these might be enchanted books," said Ella. "Enchantments I don't have yet. They could help us!" She didn't mention the fact that the only anvil she'd seen in the house had been damaged. Without an anvil, it would be tough to enchant anything. But still, she *had* to see those books!

Gran gave in. "We'll go in together," she said. "And I'll go first."

This time, Ella pushed past Rowan to be second in line. As soon as Gran opened the door, Ella smelled the familiar scents of leather, paper, and dust. Her heart ached, because the library smelled like *home*.

After they'd circled the room, making sure no illagers lurked inside, Ella ran her fingers down the spines of the books. They came in all colors and sizes, but she didn't pull any off the shelf. Because none of them had what she was looking for—the faint lavender glow of enchantment. As she rounded the last shelf, she blew out a breath of disappointment.

That's when she saw Jack slide a book into his backpack. Before she could ask what he was doing, he raised a finger to his lips. His brown eyes pleaded with Ella not to tell.

Why not? she wondered. *What did he find?*

When Gran rounded the corner too, Ella plastered on a smile. "No enchanted books here," she said. "Oh, well."

Jack shot her a look of gratitude as he zipped up his backpack and followed her out of the library.

When they'd reached the hall, Ella tugged on his arm until he stopped walking. "You'll tell me later?" she whispered.

He nodded solemnly.

When they reached the last door in the hallway, Ella held her breath. If this room was clear, maybe they could rest. Maybe she could finally let her guard down, or at least set down her heavy sword and trident.

But the room wasn't empty. A spiral staircase stood in the middle.

Gran flung out her arms. "A-ha!" she announced, bouncing on her toes like a child.

"What?" asked Ella and Rowan at the exact same time.

"This staircase leads to only one thing," said Gran. "A chest. A chest that may hold a saddle for your old grandma."

As she took the stairs two by two, Gran looked anything but old. Ella laughed and followed her up, winding around and around until they'd reached what looked like a dead end.

Sure enough, beyond the very last step, sat a chest.

Gran threw open the lid as if it might be filled with emeralds. One by one, she took out items and handed them to the children.

Bread, which made Ella's stomach growl.

Redstone dust, which Jack scooped up and added to his backpack. "For potions," he explained, when Rowan shot him a quizzical look.

Rotten flesh, which Gran pulled out with the tip of her sword.

"Ew!" cried Rowan, backing away.

But as Gran neared the bottom of the chest, her face fell. "No saddle."

Ella looked over her shoulder, hoping Gran was wrong. But a saddle isn't the kind of treasure that gets lost or hidden behind other things. Still, she wished she could make Gran feel better.

"How about these?" Ella cried, reaching for a couple of music discs at the bottom of the chest. "You could play them in your jukebox!"

When Rowan rolled her eyes, Ella's shoulders drooped. "Right." They weren't at home, where Gran could play music on her jukebox. They might no longer *have* a jukebox—or a home to return to. She tossed the discs back into the chest and closed the lid. "Sorry, Gran," she whispered.

Gran said nothing. Was she really that upset?

Ella turned to see. But the expression on Gran's face wasn't sadness. It was fear, which turned Ella's blood cold.

She followed Gran's gaze down the spiral staircase and saw white bubbles floating up, like snowflakes rising instead of falling. "What is it?" whispered Ella. "A potion?" It couldn't have been Jack's. He stood beside her, trembling.

Gran shook her head. "An Evoker cast a spell," she whispered. "To summon vexes."

Vexes?

A high-pitched horn rang out, piercing Ella's ears. Then a ghostly mob appeared up above. Then another. And another!

The first vex glowed red—blood red.

It let out an evil shriek as it swooped low.

Straight toward Jack.

CHAPTER 9

"**J**ack, look out!" Ella threw her body over her cousin, tackling him. She felt the vex attack, striking her armor.

But Ella fought back. She leaped to her feet. "Stay down, Jack!" she ordered. Then she grabbed her sword and swung at the vex, swinging again and again until her sword finally made contact. *Whack!*

The vex squealed and darted away. But another took its place!

Rowan stood beside Ella now, her bow raised upward. *Thwack!* Her arrow took out the second vex.

Gran was fighting, too. She swung at the third vex with her sword, but the vex disappeared.

"It went through the wall!" cried Jack, who was sitting up now.

Gran nodded. "It did. But it may be back."

Ella waited, barely breathing, staring at the stone

on the wall. But after a minute, which felt like an eternity, the vex hadn't come back.

"It's over!" Rowan shouted, pumping her fist in the air. "We did it!"

But Gran wasn't celebrating. "Those were only the vexes," she said. "We still have to face the evoker that summoned them." Instead of explaining, she started down the stairs, sword still drawn.

It's never over! thought Ella. *Mobs keep spawning. We can't keep up.*

Her body felt as heavy as obsidian. She sank down on the step to rest, only for a second. Then she heard it—not the shriek of a vex, but the howl of a wolf. *Taiga?*

Yes!

Ella shot up so fast, she feared she'd hit her head on the ceiling.

Taiga was alive. Her wolf was alive! And he was calling to her, telling her that it would be okay. That the war against the undead mobs *could* be won, if only they had enough help.

Then Ella heard more howling. More wolves. *Lots* more wolves.

Taiga wasn't alone. He had gathered the help they needed. And he was on his way back to her!

Ella took off down the stairs, swooping like a vex around corner after corner. She stumbled and fell, cracking her knee on the cobblestone. But she shot back up and kept running.

Down the stairs.

Through the room that held the spiral staircase.

Out the door and down the long hall.

Down more stairs.

"Gran! Rowan!" she called. "Where are you?"

She found them in the foyer, on the very bottom level. They stood still as statues, staring.

Another vindicator stood in front of them, blocking the front door. *No, this isn't a vindicator,* Ella realized. It had the same pale gray skin and big nose, but instead of a brown jacket, it wore dark robes. And when it raised its arms over its head, it didn't hold an axe.

For a second, Ella felt relief.

Then she realized what this mob—this *evoker*—was doing. Casting another spell!

As purple bubbles rose into the air, Rowan raised her bow. Gran grabbed her sword. Ella looked overhead for the vexes, but they never appeared.

Instead, the ground rumbled and growled. Fangs sprouted from the floor, snapping at Ella's feet. Like a wave passing through the foyer, the fangs shot up and then back down, over and over again.

Jack shrieked. Gran pulled him backward as another row of fangs shot through the floor.

"How do we fight them?" Rowan cried.

Gran pointed toward the evoker, as if to say, *Don't fight the fangs. Fight the evoker that summoned them!*

Ella tried. She wound back her arm, took aim, and threw her trident. But before it hit its mark, a protective circle of fangs sprung up around the evoker. The trident bounced off the snarling, snapping fangs and clattered to the ground. Rowan's arrow did, too.

But something else was growling now. *Taiga!*

Ella spun her head, trying to find him. Was he here, or still calling to her from far away?

The door! In her mind, she saw him scratching and clawing at the front door. He was here, and he desperately wanted in.

When Ella's enchanted trident soared back toward her, she grabbed it, sprang to her feet, and hurled off the trident again.

Only this time, she aimed for the window nearest to the door, hoping the force of the trident would be enough to break it.

Glass shattered, and a flurry of fur sprang through the window. Taiga's golden eyes met Ella's, as if making sure she was okay. Then he crouched low, let out a ferocious bark, and leaped over the evoker's protective ring of fangs. The evoker hit the ground with a grunt. The wolf did, too.

"Taiga!"

As the fangs that separated Ella from her wolf shrank back into the ground, she raced across the foyer. Taiga stood snarling at the place on the ground where the evoker had once been.

"It's okay!" Ella cried, dropping to her knees beside her wolf. "You killed him. You saved us. It's okay."

As she buried her face in his fur, she saw the gleam—something golden at Taiga's feet. It had piercing green eyes. "What is it?" she asked, lifting the statue so that Gran could see.

Gran gasped. "That, Ella, is a prize indeed."

"But what is it?"

"Totem of Undying," Gran said as she hurried across the foyer. When she reached for the statue, Ella handed it over. The only thing she wanted to hold tightly to right now was Taiga, whose fur was still raised in a ridge along his spine.

"It's okay," she whispered to him again. "Settle down now."

She felt Rowan's hot breath on her neck as her cousin leaned closer, trying to get a look at the gold statue. "What does it do?" asked Rowan.

Gran polished it with her sleeve. "It can bring you back from the brink of death," she said. "If you're hold-ing it when you're attacked."

"No way," said Jack, who suddenly stood beside Ella. "Can I see?"

Gran let him hold it, but suddenly Ella wanted the statue back in her own hands. Because Taiga was by her side now. He had protected her—saved her from the evoker. If she kept the statue close, could she save him, too, the next time danger struck?

As she gave her wolf another squeeze, he whined and backed away.

"What?" asked Ella. "What's wrong? Too much love?"

He trotted a few steps away and then turned, barking.

"He wants us to follow him," said Ella. "What is it, buddy? What do you want to show us?"

He led her to the front door, which was still closed.

But through the broken window beside the door, Ella saw them.

And they saw her.

A chorus of barks filled the air, and then howls. The grass outside the mansion was covered with wolves.

CHAPTER 10

"How many are there?" cried Jack, gazing out the window.

"I don't know," Ella whispered.

Dozens of wolves filled the lawn, pacing and whining. Barking and howling. Calling to Taiga.

And to me, Ella realized. Thanks to Taiga, her army of wolves had arrived. *But what do I do with them?* she wondered. She looked to Gran for help.

Gran squeezed Ella's shoulders. "You did it," she said. "You've gathered an army."

"But I didn't!" said Ella. "Taiga did!"

Gran smiled. "The wolves will follow Taiga, yes. But Taiga follows *you.*" As she tapped Ella's chest, Ella felt her shoulders stiffen under the weight of responsibility.

Then she caught the look in Rowan's eyes—a look of awe, but also envy. Would Rowan start up again about how horses were better than wolves? *I don't want to fight,* thought Ella. *Not with Rowan.*

"Maybe," Ella said quickly, "we *do* need more horses. If we're going to lead an army of wolves, I should have my own horse. Will you help me tame one, Rowan?"

Her cousin's face lit up, bright as the gold statue that Gran placed back in Ella's hands. As her fingers tightened around the Totem of Undying, she felt a rush of hope. *With my cousins, Gran, and my wolf—no, my wolves—fighting with me, how can we lose?*

But she knew they had to keep moving. Keep building their army. And keep fighting.

"Let's go," said Ella, leading the way outside to where her wolves were waiting.

*   *   *

Ella woke from a dream to morning sunlight streaming through her window, and the smell of mushroom stew. She stretched, smiled, and then bolted upright in bed.

Except she wasn't in her bed. She was on a hay bale.

And it couldn't have been morning, because the sun no longer rose in the morning sky.

"Is it noon?" she cried out, hoping her family was here in this barn, too, and hadn't left her behind. What sounded like a thousand wolves began barking from just outside the barn.

"Shh!" cried Gran, waving her hand. "Don't alarm them. Yes, it's noon. You've been sleeping for hours."

"And we made mushroom stew," said Jack, who

was curled up next to his ocelot. "I brought part of a huge mushroom back from the Roofed Forest."

Ella rubbed her eyes and stared at Jack's backpack. How could such a small boy store so much *stuff* in that pack?

Then she remembered the book he had stolen from the library—no, not stolen really, because whom did the book belong to? Those nasty illagers?

She made a mental note to ask Jack about the book—right after a bowl of hot, bubbling mushroom stew. It had cooked so long over the fire that it smelled sweet.

Ella ate it outside, bathed in sunlight, surrounded by her wolves. Taiga was the only one who sat beside her, but the others watched her with their golden eyes, as if waiting for her next command or a sign that it was time to move on.

That sign came in the form of a shadow crossing the hillside. The sun had already begun to set, and in the darkness that followed, Ella could see the fires on the horizon. Then a red-headed girl on horseback emerged from the shadows, racing toward the barn.

"Another village is burning!" cried Rowan as she slowed Victory to a trot.

Ella jumped up so fast, she nearly spilled her stew. She remembered the first village they had passed—the one that had been destroyed by the zombie siege. Gran had said it was too late to help those villagers, because the fires had been reduced to smoke, and the village to a heap of burned-out buildings.

But maybe this time, it wasn't too late. When Gran hurried out the barn door, Ella whirled around to face her.

"We need to help them!" Ella cried. "The fires are still burning. Maybe we can still save some of the villagers. And our wolves will fight with us!"

As Gran looked from the wolves to the fire-lit horizon and then back again, something shifted in her face. "We'll help them," she said. "But we have to go now."

Moments later, Ella sat behind Rowan in Victory's saddle. She no longer worried about falling off. Her legs felt strong, and she sat straight and tall. How could she not, with a wake of wolves streaming out from behind the horses?

On the chestnut mare galloping beside her, Jack readied his potions. Ella wondered what he would choose to help them battle the flames. Potion of fire resistance? Potion of swiftness? There was so much power in those tiny glass bottles. *But will it be enough?* Ella wondered.

As they neared the burning village, she could feel the heat. A river of sweat ran down her back beneath her heavy armor. When Gran motioned for the girls to dismount their horse near the cobblestone well, Ella wished she could dive straight into the well, down into the cool water below.

But the flames still burned, and the villagers needed help. When Jack offered Ella his potion of fire resistance, she drank it.

"There may still be zombies inside houses and

buildings," warned Gran. "Fight them only if you have to—to save villagers."

Ella nodded, picturing the children that might be trapped inside their own homes. When Rowan took off running, Ella raced behind her, along with what felt like a thousand wolves. She could hear them yipping and the drumbeat of their paws striking the earth.

Rowan slowed to a walk as she reached the first house. She dropped to a knee just outside a window and waved Ella to her side.

"Zombies," Rowan whispered.

As Ella snuck a glance, she sucked in her breath. The grunting mobs filled the room, bumping off walls and into each other. There were no villagers left inside. *We're too late!* thought Ella, her stomach clenching.

"C'mon!" cried Rowan, waving her on.

The next house seemed empty, but flames crept up the front door and across the rooftop. "No zombies," said Rowan. "But no villagers either. Let's go."

She was already racing away from the window, toward the next house. But something caught Ella's eye through the glass. She pressed her face closer, peering into the darkness.

There it was! Someone was pacing in the hallway beyond the living room. Someone wearing a white robe.

Zombies don't wear white robes, she told herself. *Someone's in there. Someone who needs my help!*

She banged on the window to warn the villager of the fire spreading across the house. But the figure kept pacing, as if in a trance. So Ella did the only thing she could do—she reached for her trident and swung it against the window.

As glass shattered with a horrific crash, Taiga barked, setting off a chorus of barks and whines from the wolves that wanted to help, too.

"Stay here!" Ella told them. "You'll scare the villager. I'll be right back."

But as she crawled through the open window, she felt a niggle of doubt. *What am I getting myself into?* she wondered as she tumbled headfirst into the dark living room.

As she crawled to her knees, she called out to the villager. "It's okay. I'm here to help! Your house is on fire. You have to get out!"

The figure in the hall didn't turn, but now Ella recognized the white robes of a librarian and the long dark hair of a woman. Could she not hear Ella calling to her?

Ella called out again as she crossed the room toward the librarian. Still, the woman didn't turn—until Ella was directly beside her.

Ella saw now that the woman's robes were dirty and tattered.

She heard her groan, and smelled the stink of her breath.

As the woman staggered around in a slow circle, Ella saw the putrid green flesh of . . .

. . . a zombie.

CHAPTER 11

Taiga was beside Ella in a flash, waiting for her command. He crouched, teeth bared, placing his body between Ella and the zombie.

As the zombie groaned and took a step forward, Ella reached for her sword.

"Don't hurt her!" A boy's voice rang out from a room down the hall.

But the words tumbled around Ella's mind like cobblestones. *What does he mean? Don't hurt the zombie? But I have to fight!*

Then she saw the boy poke his head through the doorway. He was about her age, with sandy-colored hair and flashing eyes. "Don't hurt her!" he cried again, sounding fierce. "She's my mother!"

Ella's chest seized—she suddenly couldn't breathe. And she couldn't fight the mob in front of her, not if this boy believed it was his mother. *Could it be?*

wondered Ella, staring at the undead mob. *Is it possible?*

The zombie staggered toward her, arms outstretched. If Ella couldn't fight, she had to run.

When she heard a *thud* in the room behind her, she whirled around—grateful to see Gran in the living room, with Jack close behind. As soon as Gran saw the zombie, she drew her sword.

Jack grabbed her arm. "It's not a zombie," he cried. "It's a zombie *villager*!"

Gran hesitated. "That's not possible."

But now Ella knew the truth. "Jack's right," she said quickly. "There's a boy in the house who says it's his mother. What do we do, Gran?" Beside her, Taiga let out a confused whine of his own.

"I can save her," Jack insisted. "I have the golden apples, remember? And splash potion of weakness." He dropped to his knees and unzipped his pack.

But a smoky haze filled the room, and Ella heard crackling from the rooftop above. "Not now, Jack. Not here—the fire is spreading!"

Gran coughed as she glanced upward. "Ella's right. We have to get out. Now, Jack!" She reached for his hand, but Jack wouldn't budge.

"What about her?" He pointed toward the zombie villager, who had begun to pace again, bumping against the walls of the tiny hallway that Taiga guarded.

And what about her son? wondered Ella. He had gone back into his bedroom, but he wouldn't be safe there—not for long.

Ella stared as a swirl of smoke in the ceiling grew bigger and blacker. Flames began to lick the edges. There was no time to think or to make a plan. There was only time to *act*.

"Taiga, help me get her out of here," she said, pointing toward the librarian. "Help me get her and her son out of the house. But don't hurt them!"

Taiga cocked his head and whined.

"I know you don't understand. Just do it, buddy. Just help me. Please!"

So he did. Taiga stepped toward the zombie villager, growling—just enough to get her attention. Then he darted toward her foot, pulling it out from under her until she fell to the floor with a grunt.

As Taiga dragged her across the kitchen, she growled and thrashed. But two more wolves had leaped through the living room window. Together, they pulled her toward the back door.

Ella sprinted down the hall to the bedroom. As she threw open the door, the boy flew off his bed and grabbed a sword from a bedside table.

"It's okay!" cried Ella. "We're going to help you—and your mother, too. But you have to come with me!"

He narrowed his eyes, as if she were the enemy. How long had he been in here, fighting for his life? She had to earn his trust. But there was no time!

"I'm Ella," she said, holding her voice steady. "What's your name?"

He licked his lips. "Sam."

"Okay, Sam. Your house is on fire. We got your mom out, but now we have to get out, too. *Right now.*"

Finally he lowered his sword and crossed the floor toward her. As she led him down the hall, past the living room, Ella held her breath. Flames flickered everywhere, as if they had just stepped into the Nether.

Her lungs burned as she raced toward the back door. She turned only once to make sure the boy was still with her. Then she followed her family and her wolves into the dark village—just as the house behind her burst into flames.

*　　*　　*

"Is it working?" Sam took a step toward his mother.

Ella quickly pulled him back. "Not yet," she said. "We have to wait." *But how much longer?* she wondered.

They were safe in the library now, where torches burned brightly, but Rowan was still out there in the dead of night. Ella's wolves were out there, too. And in the darkness, she knew mobs would soon be spawning.

Jack had used his splash potion of weakness on the zombie villager, which he insisted would help her heal. A trickle of purple liquid ran down her white robe. Now it was time for her to eat the golden apple. But how do you force a zombie to eat an apple?

"What's your mother's name?" Gran asked Sam.

"Amanda Martin," he said softly. He watched his mother's face, as if hoping she would respond.

Gran took the golden apple from Jack and offered

it to the librarian. "Mrs. Martin, I have something for you," said Gran. "Will you take a bite?"

The librarian growled, her eyes flashing like a wild animal, scared for its life.

"We're trying to help you!" cried Jack, sitting back on his heels.

Gran shushed him with a pat on the shoulder. "Sam, do you want to try?" She offered him the apple. "Your mother might take it from you."

He nodded and reached for the apple. "P-please eat it, Mom," he said, his voice shaky. "It'll help you."

Sam held out the apple halfway, like a peace offering. His mother watched him with dark, hollow eyes. She sniffed the air. Then slowly, cautiously, she reached for the apple—and took a bite.

"Yes!" whispered Jack. "You did it!" He slapped Sam on the back as if they were buddies now.

But Sam's mother started to hiss. She shuddered, pushing herself up on shaky legs, and staggered toward the door.

"Don't let her leave!" said Gran, jumping to her feet.

When Sam held out his hand to stop his mother, she forged a new path. She toppled over a shelf and stepped through the books that had spilled to the floor.

"We can't stop her!" cried Ella. "She's too strong!" It was as if the woman had drunk a potion of strength. Instead of opening the door, she broke through it with a single blow.

She started down the stairs, still shaking and shuddering. And then suddenly, she stopped. She dropped downward into a sitting position and fell silent.

"What's happening?" Ella whispered to Gran.

Jack answered. "It's working," he said. "My cure is working!"

Mrs. Martin swiveled her head, as if she had heard him. As she gazed past Jack at her son, her eyes softened. The hollow, gaping stare was gone.

Her face spread into a sad smile, and a single tear ran down her cheek.

She opened her mouth as if to speak, but nothing came out. So she licked her lips and tried again. This time, the word was barely audible, but it filled Ella's heart with hope.

Sam.

* * *

"How did you save me?" Mrs. Martin asked Gran again. "How did you know the cure?"

After a second golden apple, the color had returned to her cheeks. Ella searched the woman's face, but saw no remnants of the hostile mob that had stood in the library just a short while before—except for the tattered robe, which she pulled tightly around her shoulders.

Sam was beside her now, too, hanging on to her arm as if he'd never let her go.

Gran smiled. "I didn't know the cure," she said. "Jack did." She gestured toward Jack, who beamed with pride.

"My mom taught me," he said. "It's in her journal. I'll show you." As he pulled the book from his backpack, chunks of brown mushroom spilled out with it. "Oh, sorry." He wiped the journal clean, then flipped through the pages. "Here. See?"

As Mrs. Martin took the journal from his hands, her eyes widened. She studied the page and then flipped through a few others. "Where is your mother?" she asked.

When Jack's face fell, Gran answered for him. She quickly explained that Jack's mother, a scientist, had died during the last Uprising.

Ella glanced at Mrs. Martin, expecting to see sadness. What she saw instead was wonder. Mrs. Martin's jaw had dropped wide open.

"I knew your mother!" she said to Jack. "We were working together, trying to find a way to reset the day-night cycle."

Jack's head jerked upright. "Really? How?"

Ella leaned forward, too, listening.

Mrs. Martin shook her head. "We never found a way. Your mother had started to build something—a command block—but then . . . she didn't finish in time."

Gran nodded. "We still have that command block," she said.

Ella remembered, too—the strange block in the hidden room under the staircase! "Could we get it to work?" she asked Mrs. Martin. "Do you know how?"

The librarian hesitated. "I can help, but Jack's mother knew more about command blocks."

No wonder he's so proud of her, thought Ella, turning back toward Jack. But what was he doing? His head was stuck in his backpack. When he popped it back out, he looked discouraged. Then he lifted the pack and dumped the contents onto the rug.

Potion bottles tumbled out, along with more mushroom crumbs and a pile of golden apples. Then a book fell on top. *The stolen book!*

Ella sucked in her breath. Would Gran be angry?

Jack picked up the book as if it were a great treasure, like the golden Totem of Undying that Ella had tucked safely in her own pack. He showed off the title so that everyone could see:

Building Command Blocks: Start to Finish

Then Jack flipped open the cover. "It was Mom's, see?" he said, pointing toward the loopy signature. "She started building the command block. And I'm going to finish it!"

Silence fell over the room along with something else—hope? *Can he do it?* Ella wondered.

Sam pumped his fist, as if he believed Jack could. Jack had just saved his mother, after all.

Gran tilted her head thoughtfully.

And Mrs. Martin leaped to her feet. "You found it!" she cried. "Your mother said the book had disappeared. Oh, Jack—bravo!"

Everyone started talking at once, so loudly that Ella couldn't think.

"We have to go home and get the block!" cried Jack.

"I'll come," said Mrs. Martin. "Sam and I will come with."

"We need more horses," said Gran, who was now pacing the room.

"We need to find Rowan!" cried Ella. Had they all forgotten about Rowan?

As if right on cue, the door to the library burst open. Lucky the ocelot sprang inside, as if running from something. And then Rowan appeared. Her face was smudged with black ash, and her red ponytail hung askew.

"Zombie siege," Rowan whispered, her green eyes wild with fear. "They're back!"

CHAPTER 12

Don't mistake a zombie villager for a zombie, Gran had warned. *If you attack one, your wolves will, too.*

Ella didn't need to be told twice. She had already come face to face with a zombie villager. If she saw one again, she'd know. But would Taiga?

The wolf was at her feet as she crept into the darkness behind Rowan. Dozens of glowing eyes told her that her army of wolves was here, too, ready to fight.

When a horse whinnied, Ella froze. Gran and Jack were out here somewhere on horseback. "Are they okay?" she cried, searching the shadows.

Rowan raised a finger to silence her. "They're okay," she whispered. "Gran's a warrior, and Jack's potions are deadly. Don't you know that by now?"

Ella nodded and swallowed the lump in her throat. Gran and Jack were okay. They had to be. But as the grunts and groans of the zombies grew louder, she wondered, *Will we survive this, too?*

As they rounded a cobblestone wall, Ella saw them—masses of writhing green mobs, staggering down the street and through what was left of the houses.

Bam, bam, bam! A zombie banged against a door with his head. Ella could almost feel the ground vibrate.

"Ready to fight?" asked Rowan.

No! thought Ella. But if she waited a moment longer, the zombie might break that door down. His army of zombies would follow him in. And if any villagers were still in the home, they would never survive.

"Ready," said Ella, her voice cracking.

That was all Rowan needed to hear. She charged, letting loose a ferocious battle cry.

Taiga raced after her, then turned toward Ella whining, as if to say, *Please don't make me wait! Let's go!*

So Ella ran. She pulled the trident from her side and reared her arm back, launching the weapon toward the nearest zombie. *Thud!* It struck its mark—the zombie dropped.

As soon as the trident left her hand, Taiga snarled and attacked another green mob. And another. Then a sea of silver fur swept through the village—dozens of wolves taking their cue from Taiga, and from Ella.

The wolves tackled the undead mobs, knocking them down to the ground. They tore the zombies away from doorsteps and windowsills. As a horrifying chorus of grunts and groans filled the air, Ella longed to cover her ears. But she had to keep fighting.

When her trident returned to her hand, she spun in a circle, searching. "Taiga!" she cried. Was he okay?

The wolf sprang to her side. "Good boy," said Ella. "Stay close now."

They raced side by side through the village, dodging dead mobs and heaps of rotten flesh. When more zombies spawned behind the blacksmith shop, Ella was ready. She threw her trident again, and wolves came in droves to finish the job.

By the time she reached the edge of town, Ella's arms and legs felt heavy as obsidian. Then she saw Rowan. Her cousin sat on the edge of the well, her legs dangling off the side.

"What are you doing?" Ella cried. "Why aren't you fighting?"

Rowan smiled. "I was," she said. "But we did it. Your wolves did, I mean. Look."

Only then did Ella turn to see the path she'd left behind. Wolves speckled the lawns, the street, the courtyard, and the market area. They were licking their wounds and lying down to rest beside steaming piles of rotten flesh and other zombie drops. But there weren't any zombies left standing—not a single one.

Ella heaved an enormous sigh. "We did it," she said, resting her head on her cousin's shoulder. "We did it."

* * *

"Lucky saved us!"

As soon as Ella and her cousins were back inside

the library, Jack launched into a story. "You should have seen it. Gran heard the hiss of the creeper, and then our horse got all scared and bucked sideways."

Sam leaned closer. "Yeah, and then what?"

Jack spoke slowly, dragging out the story now that he had a captive audience. "I reached for a splash potion. But before I could even get the cork out, Lucky came from out of *nowhere*."

He paused.

"Like from where?" asked Sam. "Out of a tree?"

Jack's eyes widened. "I don't know—maybe. She just showed up, because she knew I was in danger. She chased the creeper away, quick as that." He snapped his fingers. "She saved the day!" He reached out to stroke his cat, who was fast asleep now, curled up in a circle with her head tucked under a paw.

"Cool," said Sam, eyeing up Lucky as if he wished he had a cat of his own.

Rowan rolled her eyes. "Ella's *wolves* saved the day," she argued. "Your cat chased one creeper, Jack. Ella's wolves killed at least a hundred zombies."

Ella felt heat rise in her cheeks. Rowan sounded proud of her, which was a whole lot better than being jealous. But when Jack's face fell, Ella spoke quickly. "Both of our animals saved the day, Jack. Lucky was definitely your good luck charm."

He shrugged, but he smiled.

Then Ella remembered. "Hey, did you use your potion of luck yet?"

He shook his head. "I'm saving it," he said, "for

when we need it most. Like maybe when we try to fix the command block." He glanced at Mrs. Martin, who was flipping through the book on command blocks.

She looked up. "It's just you, me, and this book, Jack. So we might need a little luck." She winked at him, but Ella saw the worry in the librarian's eyes.

Gran sighed. "What we need most of all is another *horse*—or at least another saddle, if we're all going to ride home together."

Mrs. Martin closed her book. "I can get you one of those," she said. "At the blacksmith's shop, if it hasn't been destroyed."

Gran nodded. "If I have a saddle, I can take two more on my horse, at least for a while. We won't move very quickly, though."

Rowan stood and brushed off her leggings. "So what are we waiting for?" she said. "Let's get your saddle, Gran. And then together, we can find Ella her horse." She grinned and started packing up her sack.

Ella stood, too. *Be brave,* she told herself. *You just battled a village full of zombies, so I think you can find the courage to tame a horse.*

But as she followed Rowan toward the door, her knees felt weak.

* * *

Rowan nibbled at a piece of bread, a faraway look in her eyes.

"Do you hear horses?" asked Ella.

They had stopped at high noon for a quick snack and to let the horses rest in the sunshine. Gran said it was hard for each horse to carry three riders, so they would need to take more breaks. Now Rowan seemed more intent than ever on finding Ella a horse of her own.

"I don't hear horses," said Rowan, her voice thick with disappointment. "I do hear creepers exploding— or maybe it's thunder."

Taiga lifted his head, sniffed at the air, and whined.

As the sun began to sink, Ella shivered. "It figures that a storm would roll in and ruin the only few minutes of sunshine we get." She glanced over her shoulder, wondering which direction it would come from.

Suddenly Rowan sprang up, dumping her bread on the ground.

"What?" asked Ella.

"Shh! Look!" Rowan pointed toward a clump of trees.

Ella followed her gaze, but saw nothing.

"A white horse!" whispered Rowan. "I think it's an Appaloosa. C'mon, Victory will help us catch it for you."

Ella didn't like the way Rowan said "catch it," as if the horse were a hostile mob that needed to be trapped. *Maybe it'll be tame already,* she thought, crossing her fingers.

As she climbed onto Victory behind Rowan, Jack hurried over. "Where are you going?"

"Shh!" said Rowan. "To tame a horse. Tell Gran we'll be right back."

Ella glanced at Gran, who was dishing up more mushroom stew for Sam and his mom. Part of her hoped Gran would look up now—right now—and stop them from going after the horse, or offer to come with and tame it herself. But she didn't.

Jack held up his hand. "Wait!" He dug in his backpack and pulled something out, then jogged toward Ella and handed it to her. Green liquid sloshed in the glass bottle.

"Your potion of luck?" Ella asked. She shook her head. "No, Jack, you were saving this for when we really needed it."

He shrugged. "You really need a horse." He smiled and then took off, before she could hand back the potion.

"Drink up," said Rowan with a grin. "Your horse awaits."

Ella downed the tasteless liquid in a single gulp. Then she recorked the empty bottle and slipped it into her own sack. She took a deep breath, waiting for something to happen—for a burst of confidence, or for the sun to suddenly shine down from the darkened sky. But nothing happened.

She sighed as she wrapped her arms around Rowan's waist. "Let's go."

They took off at a trot toward the trees. But as they got closer, Rowan swung her head left to right. "I don't see the white horse. Where'd it go?" She led Victory around the trees.

"There!" Ella pointed. As the white horse stepped out from behind a bush, Ella gasped.

It wasn't an Appaloosa. It wasn't a normal horse at all. This horse was nothing but bones—no flesh, no fur. And its eyes burned red.

"A skeleton horse!" cried Rowan.

That's when lightning struck—a jagged bolt that pierced the night sky. The skeleton horse lit up like a blaze in the Nether.

Victory reared with a terrified whinny. As Ella slid backward, she grabbed the edges of the saddle and hung on for dear life.

CHAPTER 13

owan pulled back on the reins, trying to get control of her horse. But Victory yanked his head away. As he reared again, Ella hung on tight.

Over Rowan's shoulder, she saw the skeleton horse. No, this wasn't the same skeleton horse—this one had a rider, a skeleton on its back! A skeleton with a *bow*.

Ella ducked, as if hiding behind her cousin's shoulder would keep her safe. But another skeleton horseman appeared to her left. She whirled around—and came face to face with another on her right.

"We're surrounded!" she cried to Rowan. "Go! Get us out of here!"

Rowan was already squeezing her legs and clucking her tongue. Victory took off like a shot, galloping across the field—straight toward Gran.

"No!" Rowan yanked her reins to the right, steering Victory away from Gran, who stood frozen like a statue. But the turn took Victory straight into the path of a skeleton horseman.

Victory stopped so suddenly, Rowan flew forward. As the horse bolted left, she slid sideways, right out of the saddle.

"Hang on!" Ella reached for her cousin's hand—and felt it slip through her sweaty fingers.

Rowan toppled onto the ground with a shriek.

But Victory kept running.

As his reins flapped loose, Ella lunged for them. She slid forward on the saddle, keeping one hand on the saddle horn as she grasped the reins. "Whoa," she cried, trying to remember everything Rowan had done to control the horse. "Whoa!" She pulled back on the reins.

Victory slowed, but as he tossed his head, Ella saw the whites of his eyes. He was terrified.

An arrow whizzed past Ella's helmet, so close she could hear the whistle. Then a skeleton horseman galloped up beside her. Another flanked Victory's left side. Ella didn't dare turn around to look for the third.

For a moment, she squeezed her eyes shut—as if that would make the mobs go away. *Think!* cried a voice in her head. *Fight back! Do something!*

She heard a vicious bark and opened her eyes to see Taiga nipping at the hooves of the horse closest to her. She turned and saw the other wolves coming, too, streaming across the field behind the horsemen.

As the wolves grew closer, snarling and snapping, one of the horsemen reared and spun away. It disappeared into the night, as quickly as it had come.

Ella turned just in time to see the second horseman galloping toward the horizon, with a couple of wolves close behind. *Yes!*

But one skeleton horseman remained—keeping stride with Ella and VIctory. Victory veered sideways, as if trying to lose the enemy, and galloped back around toward Gran and Rowan.

When the horseman followed, quick as lightning, Taiga tried to cut it off at the pass. He leaped at the skeleton jockey and bounced off the horse's bony side. As the wolf rolled across the ground, Ella's heart stopped.

"Taiga, no!" She grabbed the trident from her side and launched it sideways at the horseman.

She watched with horror as it bounced off the skeleton's helmet—and then noticed for the first time the purple glow surrounding it. The skeleton's helmet was *enchanted*. Not even her trident could penetrate that!

The skeleton drew back the string of its bow and released another arrow.

Ella ducked, praying that the arrow wouldn't strike her horse. But as she straightened back up, she watched an arrow strike the *skeleton*, knocking it right off the horse.

The skeleton fell to the ground with a grunt and shattered into a pile of bones.

"Who . . . ?" Ella swung her head and saw Rowan kneeling on the ground with her bow. As she tried to stand, her leg gave out. Rowan was hurt!

But somehow, she still saved me, thought Ella.

She pulled on Victory's reins to circle back toward

her cousin. But now Rowan was hollering something. "Go back!" Rowan called, waving Ella away. "Get the horse!"

What horse? wondered Ella. She was already *riding* it!

Now Gran was running across the field too, calling to Ella. "Get the horse!" she hollered. "We need the horse!"

Gran wasn't pointing toward Victory. She was pointing toward the white horse that was galloping away without a rider. The *skeleton* horse. And she wanted Ella to capture it.

"I don't know how!" Ella cried.

Then she saw Taiga at the horse's heels. Could he help her? She called to him—to the loyal wolf that was somehow always right there when she needed him.

"Trap the horse, Taiga! Slow him down! Help me!"

Taiga barked wildly and ran faster. He got ahead of the skeleton horse and darted in front of him. The horse stopped, confused, and reared up.

Now other wolves surrounded him, nipping at his hooves and herding him toward a clump of trees.

The horse whinnied and pranced sideways. He swung his bony head. Finally, he slowed down and spun in a slow wary circle.

By then, Ella was beside him.

Don't think about it, she told herself. *Just do it. Be brave, like Rowan. Or like Jack.*

She suddenly remembered the potion of luck that Jack had given her. Was it working? She felt a jolt of confidence shoot through her body. It *must* be work-ing. Jack was a master potion brewer.

And with luck on her side, she could tame this horse. She *would.*

Ella slid off Victory and tied his reins to a bush. Then she walked slowly toward the skeleton horse, holding out her hand.

Her entire body buzzed with fear, but she held her hand steady. She kept her voice calm and soothing. "It's alright," she said to the horse. "I won't hurt you. It's alright."

Taiga growled at her feet, but she shushed him. "No, Taiga. Be still."

As the wolf turned away with his tail between his legs, Ella took another step toward the skeleton horse. It stomped its foot, its bones rattling a warning.

It's alright, Ella told herself this time. *You drank a potion of luck. You can do this.*

She took another step, and then another, until she was close enough to reach out and touch the bony horse. It flinched away from her hand, but she stepped closer.

This time, she reached up and grasped the horse's bony back. She started pulling herself upward. As the horse jolted sideways, Ella hung on. She found a foot-hold on the horse's side and pushed herself up onto his back.

The horse reared, but Ella held her grip. "It's alright," she said. "I won't hurt you. Settle down."

The horse tried to run—it stepped this way and

that. But the wolves had formed a wall around the horse. It couldn't run. It couldn't escape.

All it could do was settle down and give in. And finally, it did.

As it lowered its head and sighed, Ella lowered her own head, resting her forehead against the horse's bony neck. *I did it,* she thought, blowing out her breath. *Thanks to Jack's potion, I did it.*

When the horse nickered, she felt a sudden wave of affection—which made her laugh out loud. Had she just bonded with a skeleton horse?

Taiga whined from the ground below.

"It's alright, buddy," she called to him. "You're my best friend—my one and only."

As she sat back up, the warmth in her chest was replaced by pride. *I did it!* she realized again. But there was no time to celebrate.

Ella heard hoofbeats and saw her family racing toward her on horseback. Now that they had three horses, it was time to go home.

It's not over, Ella remembered. *There are more mobs to fight, and a command block to build. There's more work to do. Much more.*

CHAPTER 14

"**D**oes it hurt?" Ella asked Rowan.

Her cousin had twisted her ankle during the fall off Victory. Although Gran had wrapped it with a bandage, Rowan winced when she tried to stand. She plunked back down in the grass beside Jack and Ella.

"Maybe you need some of Jack's potion of healing," Ella suggested. "His potion of luck worked for me—I couldn't have tamed that horse without it." She paused, remembering the moment when she had found the courage to mount the skeleton horse.

Jack gave a sheepish laugh. "Actually, that wasn't my potion," he said.

"What do you mean?" asked Ella, narrowing her eyes. She had felt the power of the potion. She *knew* it had worked!

He shrugged. "My potion of luck only lasts a few

minutes. I'm pretty sure it wore off by the time you tamed that skeleton horse."

Ella's body tingled from her head to her toes. "Why didn't you tell me?" she cried. "I never would have . . ." She faltered. *I never would have even tried to tame the horse without that potion. That's why he gave it to me—to give me confidence!*

Ella smiled at her cousin. "Good job, Jack. You helped me, you know. You really did."

"I know," he said, puffing out his chest. "That's what I do." Then he dug in his bag for a potion of healing to help Rowan, too.

"What are you going to name your horse?" asked Sam. He leaned against a tree, studying the skeleton horse that grazed beside Gran's chestnut mare. Along a sturdy branch above, Lucky the ocelot stretched out, licking her paws.

Ella chewed her lip. She'd been struggling to come up with a name for her horse. She closed her eyes, hoping a name would come. But nothing did. "I'm not sure," she said.

Sam sighed. "I wish I had a horse to name."

"A horse?" Mrs. Martin smiled sadly as she stepped up beside her son. "We don't even have a home of our own right now. How would we care for a horse?"

He shrugged and kicked at the grass.

"You can help feed our horses," said Ella. "I saw an apple tree over there." She pointed. "If you pick some, you can feed the horses."

That perked Sam right up. As he headed toward

the apple tree, Ella hopped up to help Gran, who was brushing her mare.

"No name for your horse yet?" asked Gran.

Ella shook her head. "Maybe it's because of this feeling I have—that the horse won't be mine for very long." As she stroked the horse's bony side, she felt him relax beneath her touch.

Gran glanced over with wise gray eyes. "Sometimes it's like that with horses."

Ella looked up. "Is that why you haven't named your mare?"

Gran nodded and gave her horse a pat. "But you never know, Ella," she said with a smile. "The right names may still come along. Maybe on the journey home."

She reached for her new saddle, but then hesitated. "I think you're going to need this saddle more than I do." She gestured toward the bony skeleton horse and chuckled. "It would be a rough ride without one."

Ella laughed. "Thanks, Gran."

Then Gran's face grew serious. "Ella, I'm going to have Mrs. Martin ride with you. I'll take Jack and his mother's precious book with me. Jack and Mrs. Martin are the only two who may be able to fix that command block. We need to get at least one of them safely back to the mansion. So if we get separated . . ."

Ella froze. "We *won't* get separated," she said.

Gran tilted her head. "We might. Rowan will have Sam—she'll keep him safe. I'll look after Jack. And I need you to protect Mrs. Martin. You need to get her back to the mansion. Do you understand?"

A thousand thoughts ran through Ella's mind. *I only just tamed my horse. I've never even ridden it really. I've never had someone ride with me. The mansion is miles away. And if we get separated—if I have to fight without you and Rowan by my side . . .* Her stomach clenched.

She wanted to look away, but she couldn't break Gran's steady gaze. Not until she answered, "Yes. I'll keep Mrs. Martin safe."

"Good girl," said Gran, squeezing her shoulder.

But as Gran placed the saddle on the skeleton horse's back, a wave of dread washed over Ella. They still had so far to go. And they were all out of Jack's potion of luck.

* * *

The fence came from out of nowhere—a barrier of splintered wood, straight in Ella's path.

"Hang on!" Ella called to Mrs. Martin, who sat in the saddle behind her. She felt the librarian's grip tighten around her waist.

When the fence was mere feet in front of them, Ella squeezed her legs and urged her horse forward. "Jump!" The skeleton horse leaped the fence effortlessly, as if it were a pebble in its path. "Good boy!"

Ella turned to make sure the other horses cleared the fence, too. Rowan and Sam came first on strong Victory. And then Gran and Jack close behind, on the chestnut mare.

Both horses made the jump, but neither was as

strong or as fast as the skeleton horse. Racing across the plains on that horse, Ella felt as if she were wearing Elytra wings. She felt as if she were flying.

Every time she turned around, her heart leaped, too. She was leading three horses that had once been wild, along with a hundred wolves streaming out behind them.

I'm a warrior, Ella realized. *I'm leading an army of wolves, just like my mother.*

The Totem of Undying was tucked safely in her pack, but right now, she felt as if she'd never need it—as if she were strong enough to take on anything that came her way. Faster and faster, she led her family through the dark night, on a horse that was quick as lightning.

"That's it!" Ella cried out loud. "That's your name. Lightning!"

As she reached down to pat her horse, he whinnied his approval. Lightning would get them safely home, Ella knew. *But do we still have a home to go back to?* she wondered. *Is it still standing?*

She clucked her tongue, urging Lightning onward.

CHAPTER 15

"Is it possible? Was no damage done?"

Gran's words were barely more than a whisper. But on the hilltop, near their home, Ella heard her loud and clear.

Gran had taken the lead on her mare, rounding the obsidian walls of the courtyard. Ella followed on Lightning. The grass all along the wall was scorched, and streaks of gunpowder smeared the obsidian where creepers had exploded. But the wall was intact, and within the courtyard, the beacon burned bright.

"Gran!" Rowan's voice rang out from the front gate on the other side of the house. "Golem's still here!"

Ella blew out a breath of relief. The iron golem had guarded their home for as long as Ella could remember. She felt Mrs. Martin relax in the saddle behind her, too.

"Thank goodness your home is safe," said the librarian. But her voice was tinged with sadness.

Because her own home was destroyed, Ella remembered.

As she helped Mrs. Martin off the horse near the front gate, Ella put on her brightest smile. "We'll show you where the command block is," she said. "You and Jack will be able to fix it. I know you will."

Mrs. Martin gazed up at the night sky. She didn't look so sure. "I hope you're right," she murmured. "I really do."

Rowan, with her sprained ankle, was already limping inside the gate and heading toward the front door.

"Wait!" Gran called. "Be careful!"

But Rowan pulled open the heavy door and disappeared inside. *She can never wait,* thought Ella with a smile—and then a prick of nervousness. What if hostile mobs were inside, lurking in the shadows?

As Ella hurried after her cousin, she reached for her trident. But as soon as she stepped inside the mansion, she was hit with the familiar scents of oak, dried lilac, and something sweet . . . what was it?

Home.

As Ella took a deep inhale, tears welled up in her eyes. Then she remembered Rowan.

She called to her cousin as she mounted the staircase, listening for grunts, groans, hissing—any sign that Rowan was in danger. At first, Ella heard nothing but the echo of her own footsteps on the stairs.

Then Rowan's voice rang out from up above. "All clear! The torches are still burning."

Ella released the breath she'd been holding and then raced up the stairs to join her.

* * *

The command block was heavy as obsidian and almost impossible to move. By the time they had brought it up the basement stairs and out into the courtyard, Ella's arms burned.

Rowan, who was too injured to help, sat impatiently by the fishpond, supervising. "Now what?" she asked, her arms crossed.

"Now we need a daylight sensor," said Jack. He had his mother's book open and lying flat on the ground. "Gran, do we have one?"

Gran was staring directly at the beacon, something she had told Ella never to do. She pointed at the bright light. "It's our only one," she said in a tight voice. "It's what turns on the beacon at night."

Silence fell over the courtyard. Ella finally spoke the words that she knew everyone must be thinking. "We can't turn off the beacon. Mobs will spawn!"

Gran nodded solemnly. "Indeed."

Mrs. Martin, who had been pacing the yard, suddenly stopped. "I may be able to disconnect the sensor from the beacon and use Redstone to keep it powered on."

Jack sucked in his breath. "Could you?"

She shrugged. "We have to try. Jack, do you have Redstone? We'll need some for the command block, too."

He nodded and raced back into the mansion. Jack always had a stash of Redstone for his potions,

Ella knew. She could practically hear him clattering down the steps to his potion-brewing room in the basement.

When Jack returned, Rowan led Mrs. Martin to the spindly vine ladder that led up toward the beacon. Her eyes widened, but she reached for the ladder. "We have to try," she said again, under her breath.

Rowan held the vine ladder taut while Mrs. Martin climbed. Ella saw the envy in Rowan's eyes. She wanted to scramble right up that ladder after Sam's mother, but her ankle wouldn't let her.

So instead, they waited. While Mrs. Martin tinkered with the beacon, Ella helped Jack carry more Redstone up from the basement. On their second trip, Ella led him back out into the courtyard . . .

. . . into total darkness.

"Gran!" Ella cried.

A torch came to life by the garden shed. "Over here," said Gran. "Help me light more torches!"

"I'm trying to fix the beacon," Mrs. Martin called from up above. "Hold on!"

Ella lit another torch and handed it to Jack. But it wasn't enough light! In the shadowy corner of the courtyard, a hissing mob spawned.

"Creeper!" Ella cried.

Taiga let loose a ferocious bark.

And an arrow whizzed overhead.

The arrow struck the creeper, who blew up with a *bang* of defeat. Gunpowder rained down over Gran's flowers.

"Got 'em!" cried Rowan, who had shot the arrow from her knees. "At least I'm still good for something."

Ella grinned. Her cousin was always looking for her next battle. *But all I'm looking for is a little light.* She glanced skyward.

When the beacon snapped back on, it nearly blinded her.

"Yes!" cried Jack, pumping his fist. He turned to give Sam a high five.

"It's not over yet," Mrs. Martin reminded them as she climbed back down the ladder—one handed. In her other hand, she held a square stone. She raised it for everyone to see. "I've got the sensor. Jack, it's go time."

Ella held her breath as Jack and Mrs. Martin placed the daylight sensor near the command block. Then they created a spiral path of Redstone leading from one to the other, just like the picture in Jack's mother's book.

As the two stepped back from their creation, Ella asked the question before Rowan could. "Now what?"

Mrs. Martin gazed up at the moon. "Now, we wait. For high noon."

"Huh?" Rowan's face fell. "That could take forever!"

Mrs. Martin nodded. "But we need that sun. When the daylight sensor picks up direct sunlight, a signal will run down the Redstone trail to the command block. I've set the block to zero—for permanent daylight. Once the sun comes up, it'll stay up. Hopefully." She crossed her fingers.

"Wait, *permanent* daylight?" Ella wondered if she'd misheard.

Mrs. Martin shrugged. "It's the best I can do right now," she said. "Until Jack or I figure out a better solution." She leaned over to muss up Jack's hair.

Gran shook her head in wonder. "Well, I can't say that I understand how it works," she said. "I just hope it does. I'll take permanent daylight over permanent nighttime any day, won't you, girls?"

Ella nodded, and crossed her own fingers—and toes.

When daylight finally came, they were settled in Gran's cozy kitchen eating warm bread and butter. As Ella reached for another slice, she realized she hadn't checked the clock for at least an hour.

But when she heard the *click!* in the courtyard, she knew she didn't have to.

Blinding light poured through the windows, a sweeping swath of sunshine that warmed Ella like a hot bath. She turned toward Rowan, who for once, seemed speechless. Her mouth hung open as she limped toward the window.

"Did we do it?" cried Jack.

Mrs. Martin covered her hands with her mouth. "Maybe," she whispered. "We'll have to wait and see."

So they waited, out in the courtyard under the magnificent sun. Lucky the ocelot stretched out on the obsidian wall, soaking up every ounce of warmth and light.

Ella held her breath, waiting for the sun to start sliding downward, for the chill of the night sky to return.

But it never did.

The sunshine was here to stay.

* * *

"We'll be back," Mrs. Martin said again as they loaded up the saddlebags of the chestnut mare. Gran had given them the horse to make the journey home.

"I thought of a name for her," said Sam, grinning from ear to ear.

"What is it?" asked Ella, eager to hear.

"Sunshine," he said. "Because she helped us bring it back. I'll call her Sunny for short."

Ella smiled. It was the perfect name. But sadness squeezed her heart. It would be hard to see Sam and his mother ride away. She suddenly felt the urge to give them something, just as Gran had given them the horse.

"Wait here," she cried. "Don't leave without saying goodbye." She raced up to her bedroom, where she had hidden a precious possession: the Totem of Undying.

Now that she was safely back at home, with the sun high in the sky above, she knew she wouldn't need it. But Sam and his mother might. They still had a long journey ahead.

When Ella stepped back outside, sunlight hit the golden statue. It had never looked so shiny!

When Mrs. Martin saw it, she sucked in her breath. "Oh, no, Ella," she said. "You keep that."

But Ella insisted. "You and Sam need it more."

When Mrs. Martin finally took it, she gazed at Ella with thoughtful eyes. "You know, your mother had one of these."

Excitement trickled down Ella's spine. "Really?" She turned to Gran, whose own forehead wrinkled with surprise. "Is it here somewhere, Gran?"

Her grandmother shook her head. "I've never seen it."

Mrs. Martin's face spread into a slow smile. "Maybe," she told Ella with a twinkle in her eye, "your mother *used* it."

It wasn't until Sam and his mother were riding away that Ella understood what those words meant. *If my mother used a Totem of Undying, then . . . maybe she never really died. Maybe my mother is still alive!*

The thought jolted Ella upright. The hairs prickled along the back of her neck. But if her mother were alive, why hadn't she contacted her? Why hadn't she come home?

Maybe, thought Ella, *she can't.*

She had helped Sam save his mother from the zombie siege. If her own mother was still out there somewhere, could Ella save her, too?

She gazed toward the horizon and made a promise, a whisper that raced across the plains like a wild horse.

If you're out there, Mama, Ella vowed, *I'll find you. I'll save you. I promise.*